Grumpy Bird

JEREMY TANKARD

SCHOLASTIC INC.
New York   Toronto
London   Auckland   Sydney
Mexico City   New Delhi
Hong Kong   Buenos Aires

When Bird woke up,
he was grumpy.

He was too grumpy to eat.

He was too grumpy to play.

In fact, he was too grumpy to fly.

"Looks like I'm walking today," said Bird.

Bird walked past Sheep.

"Good morning, Bird," said Sheep. "What are you doing?"

"Walking," said Bird.

"Nice," said Sheep. "I'll keep you company."

Bird walked past Rabbit.

"Hi there, Bird," said Rabbit. "What are you doing?"

"I'm walking," said Bird. "It's no fun."

"I could use some exercise," said Rabbit. "I'll walk, too."

Bird walked past Raccoon.

"Hey, Bird," said Raccoon. "What are you doing?"

"I'm walking," snapped Bird. "What does it look like?"

"It looks like fun," said Raccoon. "I'm coming, too."

Bird walked past Beaver.
"Hello, Bird," said Beaver.
"What are you doing?"
"Let me give you a hint," said Bird. "You do it
   by placing one foot in front of the other."
"Walking?" guessed Beaver. "I love walking!"

Bird walked past Fox.

"Good day, Bird," said Fox. "What are you doing?"

"WHY DOES EVERYONE WANT TO KNOW WHAT I'M DOING?!" shouted Bird. "I'm just walking, okay?"

"Okay," said Fox. "Let's go."

Bird walked.

The other animals walked.

Bird stopped.

The other animals stopped.

Bird stood on one leg.

The other animals stood on one leg.

Bird jumped.

The other animals jumped.

"Hey, this is fun!" said Bird.

"Come on," said Bird, who had
forgotten all about being grumpy.
"Let's fly back to my nest for a snack."

And they did.

For Hermione,
who's never too
grumpy to fly.